This book belongs to

....

Written by Alexandra Robinson.
Illustrated by Clare Fennell.

SANTA'S 12 DAYS OF CHRISTMAS

Clare Fennell • Alexandra Robinson

make
believe
ideas

Have **you** ever **wondered**
what **Santa** likes to do
when his **deliveries** are done,
and **Christmas Eve** is through?

Welcome Back!

He lands his sleigh on Christmas day, greeted by a cheer.
He's ready for a twelve-day break – it's been a busy year!

On **DAY 1** of the holidays
he throws a yuletide ball,
with disco lights, red party hats,
and candy canes for all!

On **DAY 2**, Santa takes the **train** through the **sparkling snow**.

He's off to see The Nutcracker –
his favorite Christmas show!

On **DAY 3**, jolly Mr. C

holds a **reindeer race.**

The **elves** stand by and **watch with glee**

to see who wins first place!

Finish

On **DAY 4**, Santa Claus decides to **skate** with **polar bears**.

They swirl and swish around the ice . . . and leap into the air!

On DAY 5, Santa takes his wife
to watch the town parade.
They cheer The Merry Marching Band
and praise The Dance Brigade!

On DAY 6, Santa's arctic friends invite him to the park,

where, down the hill, they sled and slide
until the sky turns dark!

On New Year's Eve, the 7th DAY,
they all watch with delight

as fireworks WHIZZ, POP,

and BANG,

filling the sky with light!

On **DAY 8**, Santa takes some **yarn**
and **dazzling** glittery gems,
then **settles** in his **chair** to knit
warm sweaters for his **friends!**

On DAY 9, Santa and the elves enjoy the frosty weather.

They play **snow games**,

build tall **snowmen**,

Day **9**

and take photos together!

On DAY 10, Santa plans to try
some recipes he's read:
three cream tarts, two fruit soufflés,
and a house of gingerbread!

On DAY 11, Santa Claus
prepares a roaring fire,
then sings some merry carols with
The Rockin' Robin Choir!

On **DAY 12** of his festive break,
he **polishes** his sleigh.

He's **ready to start** making plans
for **next year's Christmas Day!**

DAY 1

DAY 2

DAY 3

DAY 4

DAY 5

DAY 6

DAY 7

DAY 8

DAY 9

DAY 10

DAY 11

DAY 12